ROAD TRIP

Jason Halt

*Dedication to my Friend Michael K. Smith, without him I am unable
to tell you this funny and erotic story.*

Thanks
Jason Halt

ROAD TRIP

"Long, long ago in a galaxy far, far away..." That's probably how I should begin this story. But let's just say the Beach Boys hadn't yet been replaced by the Beatles and I never gave a second thought to the year-old draft card in my wallet. I was a freshman at the University of Texas and, like most out-of-town students in Austin, I didn't have a car. Those few who did either were very good at saving money in high school, or came from better-off families, or were older to begin with, and they never lacked for people wanting to be their friends. The rest of us hitched rides or hoofed it around town. (You could still walk across most of Austin in those days, and bicycles were still socially restricted to junior high and below.) Going home for the holidays, your parents would pick you up. Otherwise, the cheapest way to travel any distance was good old Continental Trailways.

Shortly before spring break of that first year, a business friend of my brother (who was nearly ten years older than me) was looking for someone reliable to drive his Lincoln Continental Mark II from San Antonio to Jacksonville, Florida, for delivery to a cousin or somebody.

The car was a baby-blue beauty, an immaculate, leather-upholstered land yacht, probably worth $8,000 or more. My brother knew I always needed funds and he vouched for me as an excellent driver (which I actually was). The upshot was that his friend offered me $100 to shepherd his Lincoln to Florida -- plus another $100 for gas and expenses and a return bus ticket. I hadn't been to Florida since a family vacation when I was nine. How could I lose? I grabbed the job.

The Friday afternoon that classes let out for break, I hitched a ride to San Antonio with a guy from my dorm; the normally ninety-minute trip took two hours because of the exodus of students headed for Padre Island and Port Aransas, but we got there. I spent the night on my brother's sofa-bed and early Saturday morning I was shaking hands with the owner of the car.

My brother had already warned me of the ground rules: No "ride along" or other passengers, no greasy food in the car, no drinks that might endanger all that leather, no speeding tickets, no night-driving, no side trips, and I should lock the car every single time I got out from behind the wheel. Well, $100 was a nice chunk of change in the early '60s and none of the owner's conditions seemed unreasonable, not with that car, not for that kind of money. By Noon, I was on the road, headed east on US-

◆ ◆ ◆

At my first pit stop, an ice house in a little town halfway to Houston, I bought a pair of mirror shades in an attempt to look cool. The Lincoln drove like a dream. I could steer with one finger and I had to watch the speedometer carefully, the engine was so huge. No cruise control in those days, of course -- no air conditioning, either -- and the mattress-like suspension, customized four-speaker radio, and tinted side and rear windows meant I had to work to keep my mind on my driving.

The best part was the other cars I passed, especially those driven by kids my own age. A casual wave and a superior smile negated their envious looks. A big blue Lincoln is a great car for improving your morale and increasing your ego.

I had hoped to completely through Louisiana before quitting for the day, but the weekend traffic in Houston killed that idea. I had just reached Liberty and was wondering if I could make it to the Louisiana line before full dark, when I saw the girl with the suitcase in her hand

getting out of an old pickup ahead.

The truck was turning off onto a side road and the girl waved to the driver and then looked hopefully back up the highway in my direction. I was less than a thousand feet away and already slow-ing as quickly as I

could without making the tires squeal.

She was about my age, blonde ponytail and bangs, black jeans, baggy red sweatshirt, and what looked like Miss Hushpuppies. Very straight-looking, probably a safe pickup. I thought about the "no riders" rule and decided it couldn't possibly apply in a situation like this. I mean, the girl was obviously in need of assist-ance.

She watched the big Continental crunch onto the gravel shoul-der and flashed me a bright smile, obviously delighted that she wouldn't have to wait for another ride. She also appraised the car as I came to halt beside her and lowered the electric window.

"Need a lift?" (A pointless formality, but expected.)

"Yup, I sure do; how far are you going?" I was instantly in love with that twangy soprano.

"All the way to Florida." I attempted a nonchalant smile. "How far are *you* going?"

"I dunno yet -- maybe Florida...." She grinned. Beautiful teeth.

I popped the door lock on the passenger side as she hurried around the front of the car, hips twitching interestingly.

She tossed her rather beat-up suitcase in the back seat and the ponytail bobbed as she hopped in the front, glancing around as she slammed the door.

"Nice car. Yours or your father's?" My head swiveled around at that, but I decided the twinkle in her eye meant it was a friendly joke and not a smart-ass crack.

To get even, I replied "Neither. I just sorta 'acquired' it." From the corner of my eye as I pulled back onto the highway, I saw the twinkle falter. She was probably wondering if I was a car thief. "The owner's paying me to get it to Florida for him," I added with a small smile and a glance through the shades. Gotcha.

She laughed. "Touche! My name's Paula, by the way."

That was too much! I cackled as I began singing in an upper register: "Hey, hey, Paula, I've been waiting for you..."

"If you're gonna make fun of me, man, you can just let me out right here!" she snapped. "I like my name!"

I waved a hand placatingly as I continued to laugh. "No, no, you don't understand! The next line is *yours* -- no lie!"

After a few seconds' hesitation, she said "Hey, hey,... Paul? You're kidding."

"Nope." I dug my wallet out of the door pocket and flipped it open to the plastic window with my Texas Operator's License. "See?" I said, passing it to her. "Paul Flowers." I was grinning like a maniac.

"Listen, I'm sorry, really. It just hit me funny. The first person I run into on this trip who's worth meeting, and we're already in a song together!"

And I began the first verse again, which had been recorded up in Fort Worth not all that many years before. Then Paula put her head back on the seat and sang: "Hey, hey, Paul, no one else will ever do..."

I was dumbfounded: Her singing voice was beautiful! Strong and clear, an alto bell made of crystal. I took off the shades and stared at her with my mouth hanging open before jerking my attention back to the road. She accepted my reaction as a compliment and we plowed into the rest of it more or less in harmony: "True love means planning a life for two, being together the whole day through,..."

We managed to finish the verse and the refrain, Paula leading and gaining strength with me following humbly in her wake. I managed not to falter but I admit to being a bit intimidated by her obvious talent.

As we finished the last "Muh-hy loooovvvve...." I braced my knees against the wheel for a moment so I could applaud. She gave me a little bow from the waist.

"I'm sure everyone asks you this," I said as I regained the wheel, "but why in the world aren't you in a recording studio somewhere? You have a *fantastic* voice!"

"Thank you -- and I wish I was. I love to sing; that's why I

left..." She paused, realizing she was saying more than she meant to, but then continued. "I, uh, left home a couple days ago. My father said I had to keep working at that damned waitress job, now that I'm out of high school -- 'not waste time and money' trying to get myself discovered." She looked at me mournfully. "But do you have any idea how much it costs to cut a demo? Even to get a good agent's attention, you have to have a demo. Or you have to know someone with enough clout and connections to get you an audition,... and I don't know anyone like that." She explained the whole thing matter-of-factly, as if repeating something she'd said a hundred times before, and probably had.

Hmmmm. "You know," I began hesitantly, "I play piano in a pretty fair little rock 'n' roll band at school. We've been doing frat parties when they can't afford a big-name group, stuff like that. Craig, our lead guitar, is the closest thing we have to a vocalist. He's okay, I guess, but he doesn't have enough volume even to carry to the middle of a dance floor."

"This band have a name?" She raised a skeptical eyebrow.

"Well, that kinda keeps changing," I laughed. "At the moment, we're the 'Colorado River Band'. We just do this for fun, you understand, 'cause we like to play together,... but we really are pretty good. And I do a *great* version of 'Great Balls of Fire', but none of us can *sing* it worth a damn."

"And you're suggesting what? That I go to Austin with you and be the girl singer with your band? At fraternity parties?" She didn't sound very impressed.

"No, that isn't quite what I had in mind. Joe, our drummer, actually does get some session work at the independent studios, the small ones, in Austin and Dallas and Fort Worth. He knows some people. I bet he could find us a place that would give us a couple hours of recording time cheap or free...." I glanced at Paula; she seemed to be listening more attentively.

"See, we've never even *considered* doing a recording. Joe's the only one in the group who has professional aspirations. But with that gorgeous voice of yours fronting us, it would be worth doing! In fact, it would be an honor to be your backup. Then, of course, when you're rich and famous, we get free lifetime concert tickets."

She laughed and nodded. "Okay, Paul, I'll think about it. I really will. But I won't quit my day job."

"Fair enough," I replied. "What day job?"

"Whatever I can find," she said ruefully.

It was after 8:00 by the time we got to Lake Charles and it dawned on me that I had a problem. If I just dropped Paula off in town and then went looking for a cheap motel, I'd almost certainly never see her again, and I didn't want that to happen. Maybe she had misunderstood.

"Um, you realize, don't you, that I'm not planning to drive all night? The owner doesn't want me driving at night, in case I fall asleep or something, so I have expense money for a motel. What--

uh,... how do you want to do this?" I'd never asked a girl to stay in my motel room before.

"If I had the money for a motel room, I wouldn't be hitching, would I?" she said a bit sharply. "You wouldn't mind me riding with you tomorrow, would you?"

"Well, no, of course not -- I'd love to have your company. But what about--"

"Look for a place where I can sneak into your room."

That sounded too good to be true. "Uh, how do you know you can trust me?"

"I don't have to." She looked me straight in the eye and suddenly raised her hand from her lap. There was a click and an open switchblade appeared in her hand. A very steady hand. I decided to believe she was capable of using it if necessary.

"Okay,..." I replied. "You made your point."

She smiled and the knife disappeared, probably up the sleeve of her sweatshirt.

I passed up the first couple of places because of the trucks parked outside; I didn't want to be awakened by semis coming and going in the middle of the night. The third place was older and smaller, only eight units, all in one row with the office at the end nearest the highway. The VACANCY sign was still on, so I pulled in and parked well away from the lights. Paula was crouched down low on the floor of the car.

I went in and told the manager, who looked about ninety years old, that I was ferrying a car and it had been a long day's drive. He gave me the room at the far end of the row, back away from the noise and lights of passing traffic.

When I moved the car down and parked in front of the unit, I cautioned my passenger to wait until I had the room door open before she made her move. The look I got made me feel a bit dumb for saying something so obvious. I got my suitcase out of the trunk and hers off the back seat, then opened the front door on the passenger side and let it remain open while I tried the key to the room. I set the bags down on the double bed and when I turned around Paula had already scuttled inside. While I went back out and locked up the car, she headed for the bathroom. But I was thinking about that double bed.

When the toilet flushed and she came out of the bathroom a minute later, looking more comfortable, I avoided the topic that was foremost in my mind by turning to the second topic, which was food.

"Looks like there's a hamburger place open right across the road," I said. "I'm gonna walk over and bring back something for supper. What would you like?"

"I'd love a cheeseburger, fries, and a coke," she said with a grin.

"I'm starving!" Then, as I turned toward the door, she said "Wait a minute,..." and rummaged in her jeans pocket, finally pulling out a moist, wadded-up dollar bill. "I don't expect you to pay for everything, man. You were getting a room anyway, but this is different, and I do have a *little* money." She held out the dollar and I took it and thanked her. That was another subject I hadn't brought up yet and I was pleased she intended to be as self-sufficient as she was able to afford. I had to make my expense funds last. I also didn't want her thinking she owed me anything; I wasn't *that* cheesy, not even at eighteen.

When I got back with two sacks that smelled of hot grease, I found Paula had shucked her shoes, socks, and jeans, and was standing in front of the wall mirror in just her oversized sweatshirt, combing out her hair.

Removing the ponytail made her seem older, perhaps older than me. Certainly more experienced about the world, I was beginning to think. But my attention was drawn by those slender, tanned legs below the hem of her red sweatshirt. I was becoming short of breath and only the fact that my own jeans were a little too tight kept my sudden erection from becoming obvious.

She turned with a smile and inhaled the french-fry aroma as she tried unsuccessfully to tug her shirt a little lower. I set the sacks on the dresser and she grabbed one and carried it to the bed, sitting crosslegged in the middle as she unwrapped her cheeseburger. I was uncomfortably aware of the crotch of her white panties peeking out from beneath the red shirt. She seemed oblivious to her display, though, or too hungry to care.

I sat around on the other side of the bed to eat my own cheeseburger; Paula was too much of a distraction for my digestion. And I still hadn't mentioned the bed, nor had she. I finally decided to act as if I were alone in the room, because I certainly wasn't going to pay for the bed and then sleep on the floor.

I went into the bathroom to take a leak and brush my teeth and discovered a damp bra draped over the shower rod. I sneaked a peek at the size tag on its back strap: 34B. Her figure hadn't been much in evidence under that baggy sweatshirt ... and now that I knew she'd taken off her bra, my briefs began to bulge again.

It was only about 11:00 but I wanted to get an early start in the morning, before the traffic built up. I came out of the bathroom prepared to switch off the lights -- but Paula had beaten me to it. She was already under the covers on the far half of the bed, curled up on her side. When I climbed in on my side, she murmured "G'night," and I responded. Then I simply lay there and waited to see what, if anything, would happen. But I was more tired than I had realized and before long I was asleep.

What woke me about 4:30 in the morning was blonde hair tickling my nose. During the night, Paula seemed to have migrated from her pillow to mine and was cuddled up beside me. She was still asleep, breathing softly, and I thought idly how nice it was to wake up like this. I turned my head to look at her and was struck by how pretty she was, relaxed with her eyes closed, and not on the defensive.

What I *wanted* to do was slip my arm under her shoulders, hold her close to me, and kiss her awake. But I figured being awakened like that was likely to lose me her company -- and, for all I knew, she still had that damn knife up her sleeve.

My slight movement apparently got the attention of her ever-vigilant subconscious, however, and she took a deep breath and yawned as her eyes fluttered open.

"'Morning," I said softly. She smiled back sleepily and stretched her arms over her head. And when she had finished stretching, one arm lay curled around the top of my head and the other had snaked across my bare chest.

"Thanks for not doing anything," she murmured. "I was a little worried I might have to fight you off last night," she continued quietly, "but you turned out to be a gentleman, I guess." I didn't tell her it had mostly been nervousness and tiredness.

"It wasn't easy," I admitted. "And it's even harder this morning, with you looking the way you look."

She gave me a dreamy look and scooted up closer. Her nose nuzzled my ear and her warm exhalation against my neck gave me goosebumps. I acted on my inclination and let one arm burrow beneath her body. She raised up just a little to accommodate it, which was reassuring.

I turned on my side to face her and stroked her downy cheek with my free hand. She pulled me into an embrace and touched my lips with her outthrust tongue. I sucked it in, played with it a little, then pushed my own tongue into her waiting mouth.

Meanwhile, my free hand had reached the lower edge of her sweatshirt and crept beneath it. I allowed my fingertips to glide up her spine and she shivered. When I tried to bring my hand around to the front, though, to get at those hidden tits, it was blocked by a sudden downward movement of her elbow.

Our lips parted and she gazed at me -- somewhat regretfully, I thought. "Let's just neck, okay? I want to kiss you a *lot* more, but no further than that -- not right now...." She touched her nose to mine to lessen my disappointment.

At the age of eighteen, I'd had sex with half a dozen girls. Usually, it was in the back seat of a car (uncomfortable, and you might get caught), once in a park (grass stains, and you might get caught), and twice on a certain girl's sofa while her parents were upstairs asleep (mandatory silence, and you *really* might get caught). Now, for the first time in my life, I'd actually *slept* with a girl, in an actual bed -- and about all I was going to get out of it was sleep. Well, with any luck, we'd be together a couple more days; who could tell what might happen?

"Okay," I agreed quietly. "I can live with that...." I withdrew my hand and smoothed her shirt back down, then wrapped both arms around her and squeezed while my mouth attacked hers. She hugged me back, arms around my shoulders. Her knees pushed lightly against mine but her thighs stayed closed.

But she made up for it by running her long tongue all around the inside of my mouth and then practically washing my face like a cat. By the time we climbed out of bed an hour later, I almost didn't need a shower, but I took one anyway.

The bathroom door had no lock and didn't want to stay latched, either, so I had to play the gentleman again while Paula took her turn in the shower. It was very tough. I didn't even prowl among the used underwear in her suitcase.

That second day on the road was quite different. I was used to the car by now, and I was becoming used to Paula. Breakfast in Lafayette consisted of two dozen doughnuts from the Spudnut and a quart of hot chicory coffee, which was about as nourishing as my road diet ever got in those days. We taped together some sheets of newspaper into an ad hoc seat cover, to keep from worrying about the leather.

Just the other side of Mobile, we made a *tiny* detour down to

Orange Beach (I know -- another rule broken), where we played in the modest surf like ten-year-olds and had a great time wasting half the afternoon. Few activities on a warm spring day are more invigorating than playing tag with a barefoot pretty girl up and down a stretch of white Gulf sand.

Even more fun was when Paula let me catch her occasionally and wrestle her into the low dunes at the back of the beach. I was careful to keep the sexual content of our romp at a manageable level and Paula laughed and shrieked delightfully when I tossed her over my shoulder and waded shin-deep into the water, threatening to pitch her in. I didn't though. I lowered her slowly to her feet and we let ourselves sink in the wet sand up to our ankles while we shared a long, slow, deep kiss. I don't think I would have noticed a tidal wave just then.

We did a lot of casual, easygoing kissing that day, both in and out of the car, and by evening we were so relaxed around each other, it was like a cross-country trip at twenty miles an hour. I found myself completely captured by Paula's quick wit and willingness to engage in verbal play. She definitely was *not* the "lil' ol' me" type.

I also played the radio a lot, turning the volume low on the Top Twenty and begging my talented passenger to sing the melody line. I'm sure she got a little tired of that, but she apparently decided it was a cheap price to pay for a ride to Florida. Besides, I was in love with that beautiful voice and I'm also sure she recognized that my adoration was sincere.

I had an ulterior motive for spending hours at the beach, though. Leaving Lake Charles as early as we had, I could have pushed hard and made Jacksonville late that evening,... which might be the last I would see of Paula. One night together just wasn't enough. She undoubtedly figured out my strategy quickly enough, but she went along with it. As it was, we squeaked through Pensacola and began looking for a motel on the other side.

This time the manager was a suspicious old cracker who kept eyeing the Lincoln and studying my out-of-state driver's license as though she expected me to break down and confess on the spot. It was the detached "tourist cabin" sort of place popular in the '30s and '40s, with a carport beside each unit. They faced the wrong way, so Paula had to climb over the hump and under the steering wheel to make her exit on the driver's side, out of sight of the office.

We'd already eaten out a light meal at a Sonic out near the Fair Grounds, so I didn't have to go out for food this evening -- which meant Paula had no time to herself in the cabin while I was gone. I was carefully polite but I also had no intention of missing an opportunity that might be promoted to intimacy. When my traveling companion went off immediately to the bathroom with hairbrush in hand, I was right behind her, fishing out my pocket comb: Together, we had enough Alabama Gulf sand in our hair to start our own beach.

Since I was (of course) paying for the room, Paula offered to let me go first in the shower this time. But I declined and sat on the side of the bed watching as she plumped down in the cabin's only chair and emptied the sand out of her jeans cuffs. As she peeled off her socks, I thought about her legs on display the previous night,... and how cute her ponytail was, and her sweet smile in bed that morning and the ferocious way she had kissed me then, and the soft giggles she had hidden in my ear and the gentle kisses we had exchanged in the dunes at the beach.

And tomorrow, around lunchtime, I'd be delivering the car while Paula went off to wherever to seek her fortune. I didn't kid myself that I was in love or anything so serious, but I was going to miss her company in a very big way. I was also honest enough to recognize my unsatisfied horniness for what it was. I wasn't looking forward to that solitary bus trip back to Texas.

"Paul,... what's the matter?" Her quiet voice snapped me back. She was sitting there with a bare foot across her knee, wiggling her toes and searching my face with an expression of genuine concern. I was embarrassed at being caught mooning over her, but I discovered I couldn't lie to her face. I sighed and shrugged.

"I was thinking that I probably won't ever see you again after tomorrow. Less than two days and two nights, and I guess I'm going to miss you, Paula. Hell, I'm going to miss you a lot! Just feeling a little sorry for myself, is all." I put on a not-very-successful brave smile. She looked at me another few seconds and then got up and sat again close beside me. She squeezed my hand and leaned against my shoulder.

"I'm touched, Paul, I really am. You're a nice guy and I've sure enjoyed the trip with you. I even like to sing for you,... just for you," she added, and leaned closer to kiss me lightly on the cheek. That was supposed to make me feel better, but it didn't. It only made me more acutely aware of our impending separation. But I kissed her back and nodded. Her gaze lingered on me for a moment longer. Then she got up from the bed.

"Well, I'm going to go take my shower." And she stepped into the bathroom and unzipped her jeans even as she pushed the door closed. I just sat where I was, listening to the shower curtain rustle and the old faucets being turned, and the shower head spitting. Damn.

After about five minutes, though, I heard her voice from the bathroom: "Mumble mumble, Paul?"

I got up and cracked the bathroom door. As the steam clouds drifted out, I said "What? I'm here but I didn't understand what you said...."

"I said 'Would you come in here, Paul'?"

I understood *that* well enough and stepped into the bathroom. The humidity was already 100% and I could barely make out her figure through the cloudy old plastic shower curtain.

"Uh, yeah? What's the problem?" Her shadow stopped moving and then her wet, shiny face appeared around the end of the curtain.

"What are you waiting for, an engraved invitation?" she asked with a mock-stern expression. "I invited you to join me, man. You can scrub my back and I'll scrub yours." She disappeared behind the curtain again. "Jeez, you can even leave your clothes on if you want," she laughed. I set a new record for getting naked from a standing start.

It was the best shower of my life to that point. There's something innately romantic and sexy about encountering a wet, gleaming body through a fog of hot steam. Paula was cute, pretty, whatever -- but in the shower she became sultry and alluring.

She handed me a wash cloth and a miniature bar of soap and said with a grin, "Why don't you lather me up...?" So I made the soap travel up and down her arms and her thighs, across her shoulders and back, and then all over a truly delicious pair of tits. They were the perfect size to cup in my hands and they were firm and responsive to my touch. When my palms covered her breasts and I pinched her nipples a little, Paula leaned into me and put her head back so I could nibble on her throat.

That also pushed my enthusiastic cock against her groin and she reached down without hesitation and squeezed. My mind was pounding along, trying to figure a way to screw this gorgeous girl while standing on the slick porcelain. Or should I wait until we were in bed? But Paula felt the trembling in my hands; she put her own hands firmly on my waist and looked me in the eye, up close.

"Paul, I'm sorry -- but we need to agree on something, like we did this morning...." She kissed me quickly, lightly. "I trust you or I wouldn't have invited you in here. I know you won't try to push me into something. The thing is--" She paused and took a deep breath. "--I don't want to fuck. It's not you, man -- it's *anybody*.

This is really nice, in here with you, and it's really sexy, and you *know* you're making me horny as hell!" She stopped to kiss me again. "And I really do like you, Paul. But can we keep this to just mouths and hands? Please?"

The pleading in her voice was obvious and I knew if I didn't agree -- and stick to it -- she'd push me out of the tub right now. Well, what I had now was a major improvement over that morning's lingering frustration.

I cleared my throat. "Question: Can we do whatever we *want* with 'mouths and hands'?" I raised my eyebrows and pursed my lips judiciously. If my hands hadn't been still engaged in massaging her breasts, I would have folded my arms for dramatic effect.

"Idiot." She leered and kissed me again. "Of course we can. I was just thinking of all the interesting things we *could* do...." She squeezed my cock again and pulled upward on it -- a marvelous sensation. And she was right: There were *lots* of things one could do with just mouths and hands.

I temporarily abandoned Paula's breasts and slid my hands around and down to stroke and squeeze than lovely little ass. I planted myself and lifted her up on the balls of her feet so I could bend a little and wrap me tongue around her nipple. She moaned softly and her fingers sifted through my hair.

"Mmmmm... I love that... Use your teeth there -- just a little!" She inhaled sharply as I tugged at her nipple with my incisors and let it bounce back; she tried to wrap my head up completely in her arms. After a few minutes, just as I was beginning to develop a crick in my back, Paula said, a little shakily, "Oh -- Paul,... Ahhhh -- that's enough... You keep this up and I'm gonna come too quick...!" Her fingers tickled my ears. "Besides, it's my turn, lover." The intimate pet name sounded very nice indeed.

Her water-slick body moved down mine and she settled into a hunker, steadying herself with one hand behind my knee and taking control of my cock with the other. And it was my turn to wind my fingers through her hair as she rubbed the head of my cock against her nipples and grinned up at me playfully. Then she guided it up her breastbone, her throat, under the curve of her chin, to the edge of her lower lip,... and stopped.

The old cracker in the office was going to find me in the bathtub in the morning, I thought -- dead of a lust attack and a terminal erection. I clutched at her head and choked out, "Christ! Don't stop!"

Paula's throaty laugh caused a small breeze in my pubic hair and made my kneecaps tingle. She did a quick hawklike swoop and engulfed my penis. A stab of pleasure punctured my chest as her tongue prodded the tip and her fingers teased my testicles. I was, very suddenly, so completely aroused I would cheerfully have humped that Lincoln out in the carport. I desperately repeated the rules to myself, under my breath -- "Hands and mouths, hands and mouths!"

Looking down at the top of her head, at the drops of water refracting her damp blonde mop, I was struck again by how much I was going to miss Paula. Not fair, I complained silently. It's just not fair. Why do you always meet fantastic girls under the most impossible circumstances? I knew I'd never meet anyone to rival Paula in Freshman English: That just wasn't the way the world worked.

My gonads weren't worrying about the future, though. They were tightly focused on the nerve endings in my straining cock. As Paula continued to suck and squeeze, I could visualize my climax rising, like the mercury in a thermometer in July. Whether it was the tensing of my groin muscles or the inarticulate sound I made, she timed it perfectly. She let my cock *POP* from between her lips and tucked it again under her chin just as my long-postponed orgasm exploded.

I reflexively pressed her face against my stomach as I trembled through my climax; she quickly turned her head so she wouldn't smother and snuggled her cheek against me instead. She didn't say anything but I had the distinct feeling she felt flattered by my rapid eruption. I wasn't thinking too clearly just then, but I was vaguely surprised. I couldn't imagine any guy *not* being overcome by such an excitingly sexy girl.

As I caught my breath, I got my hands under her arms and lifted her back to her feet. My semen ran in rivulets from her throat down over her "perfect handful" breasts and it smeared across my chest as I hugged her and kissed her with more passion than I had ever felt for anyone. She squeezed me in her arms just as tightly, and it seemed again that there was something besides passion in her movements.

"What am I gonna do without you?" I asked a bit hoarsely.

She held my face in her hands and gave me a serious look. "You're going to do just fine without me, Paul, and you know it."

I didn't feel like being reasonable or realistic and I shook my head. "Civilization as we know it will end two seconds after I have to say goodbye to you, Paula," I said softly, and smiled as I smoothed her drenched hair.

She put her hands lightly on my chest and looked down at them. I thought she was blushing but we were both pretty red-faced already, from exertion. It made her even more desirable and I lifted her chin and kissed her again, more gently this time. She seemed to flow into it. Maybe we really were in love, at least for a minute or two.

Then our lips parted and our hands got busy again. Paula had given me my climax and I had to do at least as much for her. I lathered up one hand again and cupped her pubic mound, sliding over the silky blonde thatch and letting my fingertips rest at the very top of her cleft. Then my middle finger moved slowly downward and Paula held onto my arm and humped forward a little. My finger changed course slightly, to detour around the ridge of her clitoris, and she made a small "ummff..." sound of frustration and teased my arm with her nails.

My finger slid in farther, awash in the moistness of her, until all three joints were hidden. She was hanging on my shoulder, cheek against my arm, thighs on either side of my knee -- a hot, clinging presence that I relished.

A second finger stealthily joined the first and when I played scissors with them her hips squirmed. I dragged my fingers slowly upward between her labia until I had her clit cornered. Then I began gently caressing, stroking, and tweaking the hard little bud. Her anticipation had made her especially sensitive and her twitches and tiny jerks meant I was getting to her.

I gradually increased the pace and Paula moaned in the back of her throat and let her eyelids flutter shut. She was practically trying to climb my leg and both her hands were clutching and moving about restlessly. My cock was becoming erect again, brushing against her smooth upper thigh. I suspected I would be able to maneuver her body around while she was in the throes of masturbation and ease my cock in next to my busy fingers -- but she had played fair within the limits she had set, and for me to do otherwise would be cheating.

After a short time, my fingers were moving in and out, up and down so rapidly my hand was becoming stiff. Paula's grip on my arm had cut off most of the circulation and her forehead was pressed hard against the corner of my shoulder. She whimpered loudly, nearly sobbing, and her whole body was shaking. She was poised nearly on tiptoes, knees rattling together, her crotch thrusting against my hand, then retreating, then returning.

My other hand, which had been steadying her waist, had slipped down to stroke and squeeze her ass again. We were also beginning to run low on hot water -- though Paula was generating so much heat herself, I doubt she noticed. My cock, having worked itself to a high pitch from the friction of her thigh, jerked and sent a modest quantity of semen dribbling down her leg.

If we kept this up much longer, one of us was going to faint. Maybe both. I made a two-finger fist and shoved it up into her cunt several times, a little more roughly than I had intended. Her

whimper became a squeak and she went rigid for a few seconds --
and then boneless. I had to quickly wrap my arms around her to
keep her from falling.

I held her up until she began to recover and get her feet under
her; even then she was shaky. Finally, she draped her sweaty
arms over my shoulders and stared at me with gleaming eyes. As
her arms tightened around my neck, drawing our faces and over-
heated bodies closer together, she said, "Paul, you'll never know
how much I *wanted* to fuck you ... and I don't know if I could
have made myself stop if we'd started." She smiled so brilliantly,
my pupils contracted. "I guess this is one time the guy had more
self-control than the girl. Thank you...." And she kissed me very
sincerely indeed. My animal self was bitching at me for not taking advantage of her; could she have blamed me, after all? But my
Jiminy Cricket side was pleased that I had maintained Paula's high
opinion of me.

She stepped under the shower and shivered as the chilly spray
splashed off her head and shoulders. I laughed at her tortured expression and she grinned and swatted at me.

"Don't forget your chin, lover; it's a little sticky..."

"Oh, I can fix that," she laughed and yanked me under the shock-
ingly cold water with her. I *whooshed* and then hugged her
again as she said "*You* put it there, *you* wash it off!"

So I splashed water across her throat and breasts and enjoyed
the smoothness of her surfaces as I cleaned up the results of our
limited love-making. Then I did a couple turns under the shower
head and rinsed the accumulated sweat off myself. There was no
point in trying to soap up in cold water.

Half an hour later, we were under the covers, both of us still
naked, which I took as an additional sign of her trust. We were
still a little chilly, even in northern Florida in April, and we snuggled happily against each other. It was a little early for bedtime,
but the drive and our exertions in the shower had taken their toll,
and we dosed off soon after.

I awoke once in the night for a call of nature and found Paula's leg draped over my own and her head resting comfortably on my chest. I would never have moved except for internal pressure.

When I finished and came back to bed, she was about ten percent awake -- just enough for her hand to be searching restlessly across the pillow for me. I slipped back under the covers and slid my arm under her head again. She smacked her lips in satisfaction and grunted sleepily as she scooted up against me. I lay there a little while just looking at her face, her tousled hair, the curve of her arm. I stroked her fingers very, very lightly and she squeezed a fistful of the sheet.

I knew we'd have to part tomorrow and I knew it couldn't be helped, and I felt very sad. And I fell asleep with that thought in my mind and waded through a fragmentary dream in which I was riding the bus (or was I driving it?); we stopped out on the highway in East Texas to pick up a rider -- who, of course, was Paula, but she didn't recognize me. I awoke just before sunrise blinking back tears.

We both tried to act businesslike as we got ready to leave; it seemed easiest not to even mention what the day held for us. I had seen a big drive-through carwash -- big enough to handle trucks, with vacuum hoses and everything -- and I wanted to stop and tidy up the Continental before delivering it to its new owner.

We got there early enough that we didn't have to wait and I went through the vehicle, hood ornament to tailpipe, vacuuming and brushing the floor, wiping down the upholstery and the dashboard, running a borrowed chamois over the exterior chrome. I wanted that car to look new when I relinquished it.

Paula helped out willingly until we were almost finished and then laughed and said she had to make a pit stop herself. I wondered if she was planning to disappear on me, but I spotted her bag standing on the hardtop by the rear wheel. And then she was back and there was no further reason for delay.

The address I was headed for was out near Jacksonville Beach, beyond the end of Atlantic Boulevard somewhere (no surprise there; anyone who could afford this car could afford a beach house), and Paula watched for street names as I watched the growing rush hour traffic.

We located the turnoff but as I flipped on the blinker and slowed down, Paula grabbed my arm. "The beach is only a couple blocks on, Paul. We're still pretty early. I want to see the ocean with you, just once -- please."

I glanced at her; prolonging the farewell wasn't go to do either of us any good. But I stepped on the accelerator again and three minutes later we were parked at the end of a short, unpaved road overlooking a broad, not terribly clean stretch of sand. I suspected the quality of the beach improved whenever a hurricane came through.

We got out and walked slowly down to the water's edge, and then strolled a little way to the south; someone was running a dog off in the distance to the north, but it was too early for many people this far out. Paula's arm was linked through mine and neither of us said anything for a few minutes. Finally, her arm squeezed mine and we stopped.

"I have to tell you why," she said. "I owe you that, I think." I didn't have to ask 'why what'.

"Paul, you're only the third guy I've been naked with. The first time was on my sixteenth birthday and it doesn't really count. Neither of us knew what we were doing and we blew it; we never really had sex." Why was she telling me this? I hadn't thought she *was* a virgin.

"Then, starting a little while after that, there was a guy I went steady with for six months. I lost my virginity because I was in love with him -- I guess. I don't know, now. He was a couple years older than me and he had a lot more experience, and I suppose I was 'dazzled' or something. But one night I was over at his place and we got kind of drunk and he shoved me down on his bed, and--" She paused and took a deep breath, and looked down at the sand.

"He wouldn't stop when I begged him to. We'd had sex before, several times, and I don't know whether it was my fault or if he raped me or what. He didn't hit me or anything. But he wouldn't stop. And when I sat and cried afterward, he just told me to shut up, that he was entitled to it because I loved him. I didn't see him any more after that."

I lifted her chin and she looked at me reluctantly with tear-sparkled eyes. I put my arms around her and just held her for a couple minutes; I couldn't think of anything to say and I almost felt like crying with her.

"Then, for nearly a year, I hardly even dated -- and I didn't make out with the guy when I did go on dates. I kept to myself and they stopped asking me out. And then you picked me up on the high-way, just by accident."

She peered at me earnestly and touched my face. "And you were so nice to be with, I was able to relax. You didn't try to pull any-thing -- even though I knew you wanted to do it with me. I'm not blind, you know." She smiled and I smiled back.

"I wanted to do it, too. I wanted to have sex with you, Paul. But it still scared me and I had to come back to it a little at a time. But now we're *out* of time," she added. "Almost."

She dug down in her front pocket and pulled out her closed hand. "While you were finishing up the car this morning, I snuck into the men's room there; they had one of those machines." She held out her open palm: Two circular red foil packages with "SHEIK" printed on them. "Two for fifty cents. We can use at least one of them."

My brain was cranking up like a dragster as I glanced around. There was no cover, no dunes of any significance, not here. She tugged at the front of my shirt and put her lips next to my ear. "I want to screw in the Lincoln," she whispered. "And I want to do it right now."

The car wasn't really hidden from view but it wasn't that obvious, either. I wondered what Paula would have done if we'd had to park in a lot full of picnicking families. Maybe she didn't care. We were both strangers here and we'd be leaving shortly, anyway. Suddenly, it just didn't matter. This was a farewell I hadn't expected and I wasn't going to spoil it by worrying about the location.

We slid into the back seat and locked the doors. With the tinted windows, maybe no one would even notice that the car was inhabited.

Paula had her sweatshirt pushed up and her bra unhooked before I could even unlatch my belt. And by the time I had my jeans and my shorts pushed down, she'd already stripped herself naked below the waist.

The leather creaked as she got up on her knees and climbed across my lap. My cock was already coming to attention and she shot me a wicked look as she took it in hand and brushed the tip of it across her moist cunt. She eased it into herself just the smallest bit -- just enough to let me feel the real her and to complete my erection in a hurry.

I ripped open the foil and started to roll the prophylactic down over my cock, but she pushed my hands away and did it herself, never breaking eye contact as she smoothed it into place. Then she lowered herself onto me, nibbling at her lower lip as she sank down. She flexed her internal muscles and little jolts of electricity spread through me as I slouched down on the seat.

My hands rested on her hips to guide her movements, but that wasn't necessary. She wanted this as much as I did and she held her shirt up out of the way and leaned over so I could get my mouth around her tits. I cupped her ass in my hands and massaged her vibrant flesh as we moved. Then her hands were clutching my shoulders, fingers digging in, as she moved in all directions to make maximum contact.

It didn't last more than ten minutes, which was as long as I could hold out without coming. Under the circumstances, I don't know whether she had an orgasm or not, but she undeniably enjoyed the experience. I held her ass in a tight grip and raised her up and jammed her down until I felt as though I would explode. And when I came, gasping, she squatted down as tightly as she could, cramming as much of me as possible into herself.

She was breathing loudly through her mouth and her ponytail had come unbound, which made her shining hair form an incandescent halo about her face. She was absolutely beautiful.

When it was over, she hugged me tightly around the neck and we simply sat there, my cock slowly withdrawing by itself, and tried to remain one body for a little while longer.

Twenty or thirty minutes later, we turned into the circular drive of a large, palm-shaded house and I parked carefully and set the brake. Paula got our two suitcases out of the trunk while I went and rang the bell.

The guy who answered and came out to look at the car was pleasant enough; a somewhat younger-looking version of the previous owner. I introduced Paula as my sister, along to keep me company, and he walked around the Lincoln and nodded his approval at its condition. When, at my request, he climbed in to check on the leather interior, he sniffed the air and seemed a bit puzzled. Paula grinned and nudged me.

We went inside so he could write out a receipt of delivery and pick up his wallet and keys: He was going to drive us back into town to the Continental Trailways station. Paula and I even drank a couple of big glasses of Florida orange juice while we waited in his kitchen.

Since Paula was my "sister" for a little while, I didn't think I should hold her hand in the front seat on the way back into Jacksonville -- but she kept finding subtle ways of touching my leg, moving her foot against mine, and generally holding my attention.

The new owner of the Lincoln dropped us off in front of the bus station and shook my hand,... which came away with a folded twenty in it. I hadn't really expected a tip, but he smiled and said "You did a good job, kid," so I was happy to accept it.

We went in and checked the schedule on the wall. The next bus to Houston was leaving in about two and a half hours, but I noted that the New York bus was pulling out in less than an hour. Paula had said something vague about being dropped out on US-1, but I had shushed her. Now she was obviously wondering how she would get back to the highway to wait for a ride.

I told her firmly to sit down and keep an eye on the bags while I got my ticket. When I came back and handed her a New York ticket as well, she got all flustered and tried to protest. It had taken most of my profit from the trip after paying for my own ticket, but I didn't care about that. I sat beside her and held her hand and tried to explain it to her.

"Paula, I want you to be someplace where you can find work while you get your singing career organized. The only way I'm going to be satisfied is when I hear you on the radio in a year or two. You can't waste talent like that; I just won't allow it." Then I slipped my hand down between us where no one could see and tucked the twenty dollar tip in her front pocket, along with a slip of paper with my Austin address. Her mouth opened but I put my other finger to her lips.

"You're going to need that more than I will," I insisted. "I'm just going back to school, to play piano at frat parties and get my degree. You're going out into the real world, and you'll have to learn not to turn down opportunities." I tapped her pocket. "That's an opportunity."

She sat there looking at me with an expression I'll remember all my life. Her mouth trembled and the tears welled out and trickled unheeded down her cheeks. Then she put her hand on the back of my neck and pulled me into a kiss that made the entire bus station disappear.

◆ ◆ ◆

And that's the end of the story. I put Paula on the bus and she grabbed a window seat so we could gaze at each other as the driver pulled out. And then she was gone. I went back inside and sat and moped for another hour and a half until my own bus left. As I had expected, it was a long, lonely trip back to Texas.

About two weeks after I returned to class, I received a postcard from Paula -- a photo of the Empire State Building -- telling me she'd made it safely to New York, had found a job in a record store, of all places, and was staying temporarily at the YWCA. She was beginning to make the rounds of agencies and hoped to find the right connection soon.

There was no return address on the card -- and it dawned on me, very belatedly, that I had never even discovered her last name. Jesus. I thought of her all the time, but only as "Paula."

I kept on playing piano, just for entertainment, and I got my degree. I never heard Paula's voice on the radio, at least not on the pop stations I listened to.

I started graduate school as a Teaching Assistant and met a girl who worked in the departmental office; we began seeing each other and were married seven months later. We found a small apartment surrounded by other impoverished students and we were very happy (and we still are).

That fall, I happened to be watching our little black-and-white TV while grading excruciatingly bad freshman papers, when I suddenly recognized the voice singing the jingle for a commercial: It was Paula's lovely alto. It only ran for maybe thirty seconds during the sales pitch, but it was her.

I borrowed a tape recorder and hooked it up next to the TV, and I sat and watched stupid shows on the same station for an entire weekend, which alarmed my poor wife a bit. My finger was poised over the RECORD button at every commercial break and finally I was successful. The jingle ran again and I managed to get the whole thing.

Thereafter, I heard her voice singing background on several other commercials for assorted major products. She hadn't made the big time, but she was singing and probably making a good living at it, even if no one knew her name but me.

I still have that fuzzy old tape. My wife wisely ignores it, and the kids probably think I'm crazy, but I take it out of its box once in a while and listen to it.

And I remember the Lincoln and making love on the leather upholstery, overlooking the beach outside of Jacksonville, Florida.

END